Peppa's PERFECT Day

By Courtney Carbone
Illustrated by Zoe Waring

 A GOLDEN BOOK · NEW YORK

Licensed by
Hasbro eOne

This book is based on the TV series Peppa Pig. Peppa Pig is created by Neville Astley and Mark Baker.

PEPPA PIG and all related trademarks and characters TM & © 2003 Astley Baker Davies Ltd/Entertainment One UK Limited. HASBRO and all related logos and trademarks TM & © 2021 Hasbro. All Rights Reserved. Used with Permission.

www.peppapig.com

Peppa and George are having fun playing dinosaurs and dollies.

"Children!" Mummy Pig calls from downstairs. "There is a special surprise for you!"

"Hooray!" yells Peppa.

She and George run downstairs to see what the surprise is.

Knock, knock.

The surprise is at the front door.

"Who's there?" Peppa asks.

"Granny and Grandpa Pig!" they answer.

Granny and Grandpa Pig are all wet from being out in the rain. But Peppa and George give them big hugs anyway.

"Come in and sit down," Mummy Pig says. "I just put out some tea and cookies."

"Lovely!" says Granny Pig.

Granny Pig takes a large square book out of her bag. "Do you know what this is?" she asks.

"It's a photo album!" Peppa exclaims.

"That's right," Granny Pig replies.

Granny Pig opens the book to the first page.
It is full of wonderful photos!
"Is that me?" Peppa asks, pointing to a
picture of a young pig.

"That's Mummy Pig when she was your age,"
Grandpa Pig says.
　"She looks just like me!" Peppa says with a laugh.

Peppa sees a picture of Granny and Grandpa Pig's wedding.

She sees a baby picture of Mummy Pig and Auntie Dottie.

She sees a picture of Grandpa Pig and Granddad Dog on a fishing trip.

But Peppa's favorite picture of all is a close-up of Polly Parrot!

Peppa likes how each picture shows a special day with family and friends.

This gives her an idea! She wants to tell Granny and Grandpa Pig about her special memories, too.

Peppa runs upstairs and returns with a large box
of photographs. The box is almost as big as George!
"Can I add them to the album?" Peppa asks.
"Of course!" Granny Pig replies.

Peppa's first photo shows a glass building
with beautiful flowers and plants.
"That looks like the Botanical Gardens,"
Granny Pig says.

"This was my favorite day ever," Peppa says. "We saw wildflowers, cacti, rain forest plants— even a muddy puddle garden!"

"That *does* sound like a very special day," Granny Pig agrees.

George reaches into the box and pulls out another photo.

Peppa, George, and Suzy Sheep are making funny faces in a photo booth. There is even a silly picture of Daddy Pig!

"That was the day we all went to the shopping center," Daddy Pig says.

"We saw my best friend, Suzy Sheep, there!"
Peppa remembers. "I actually think *that* was
my favorite day ever."

"Mine too!" says Mummy Pig.

"But you were at the spa the whole day,
Mummy," Peppa says.

"I know!" she replies with a laugh.

Peppa pulls out a picture of her friends in front of a large cheesecake.

"We went to Cheese World for Mandy Mouse's birthday party!" Peppa tells Grandpa Pig. "There was a cheese river, a cheese mountain, a cheese castle, and a cheesecake!"

"Wow," says Grandpa Pig. "I want to have my next birthday there."

"Me too," says Granny Pig. "It sounds delicious!"

"It was!" Peppa replies. "In fact, I just changed my mind again. *That* was my favorite day ever!"

Everyone laughs.

"You know, Peppa," says Mummy Pig. "It's
okay if you can't pick just one favorite day.
They were all very special."

"Actually, Mummy," Peppa replies, thinking.
"I know which day is my favorite of all. . . ."

"Which one?" Grandpa Pig asks.

"My favorite day of all is . . . this one!" Peppa
exclaims. "Because I get to remember these fun
memories with all of you!"

"That's wonderful, Peppa," says Granny Pig, smiling.

Granny and Grandpa Pig help Peppa and
George paste the pictures into the photo album.
"There," Grandpa Pig says. "All done."
"Just in time—the sun has come out,"
Granny Pig adds.

"Look!" Peppa says.

She points to the window. A large rainbow stretches across the sky.

"Let's go outside and take a picture," says Peppa. "Then we can add this day to the photo album!"

"Great idea, Peppa," Daddy Pig says. "I'll get my camera."

Everyone puts on their jackets and rain boots.

Peppa and George run outside to find the perfect spot for a photo. "Over here, everyone!" Peppa calls. "This spot is the muddiest!"

Daddy Pig sets a timer on his camera. He presses the start button, then runs to join the group.

"Three . . . two . . . one . . . Now!" Peppa exclaims.

Splash!

Peppa jumps into the muddy puddle just as the camera flashes.

Everyone laughs and joins in the fun.

What a perfect day! What a wonderful memory!